Published by Princeton Architectural Press
202 Warren Street, Hudson, New York 12534
www.papress.com

First published in France under the title *Quand je serai grand*
© 2016, helium / Actes Sud, Paris, France.
Published by arrangement with Debbie Bibo

ISBN 978-1-61689-602-7

The book was illustrated by the author using watercolors.

For Princeton Architectural Press:
Acquisitions Editor: Rob Shaeffer
Editors: Amy Novesky and Nina Pick
Typesetting: Benjamin English

Special thanks to: Ryan Alcazar, Janet Behning,
Nolan Boomer, Nicola Brower, Abby Baxter, Abby Bussel,
Jan Cigliano Hartman, Susan Hershberg, Kristen Hewitt,
Lia Hunt, Valerie Kamen, Simone Kaplan-Senchak,
Jennifer Lippert, Sara McKay, Eliana Miller, Wes Seeley,
Sara Stemen, Marisa Tesoro, Paul Wagner, and
Joseph Weston of Princeton Architectural Press
—Kevin C. Lippert, publisher

Library of Congress Cataloging-in-Publication Data
available upon request.

When I Am Big

Maria Dek

Princeton Architectural Press

New York

When I am big, I'm going to be really big, like **1** big giant!

I will ride a bicycle that has **2** horns. Toot toot!

I will tie my shoes all by myself, and I will make 3 knots with big bows.

I will have 4 hats for my adventures to the south, the north, the east, and the west.

I will eat a cone with **5** scoops of ice cream for lunch.

I will put **6** spoonfuls of sugar in my coffee.

I will have 7 different jobs, one for each day of the week.

But my favorite job will be walking animals.

I will have **8** of them, and I will teach them how to do tricks.

I will jump over **9** puddles. All of them at once!

I will dash down **10** ski slopes.

I will play a trumpet with **11** buttons.

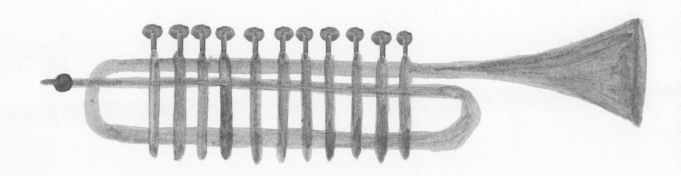

And I will be the loudest of our **12**-member band!

I will live in a tree house with 13 windows

that look out on a volcano, the North Pole, and the Moon.

I will climb **14** branches to get to my tree house.

It will be so big that a family of 15 bears will fit inside.

I will race through the forest like the wind. **16** tall trees will lead the way.

I will build a roller coaster that has 17 cars and is **17** miles high.

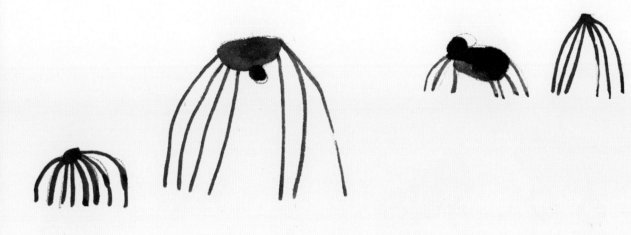

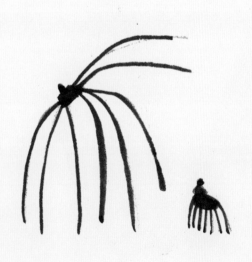

I will have **18** pet spiders.

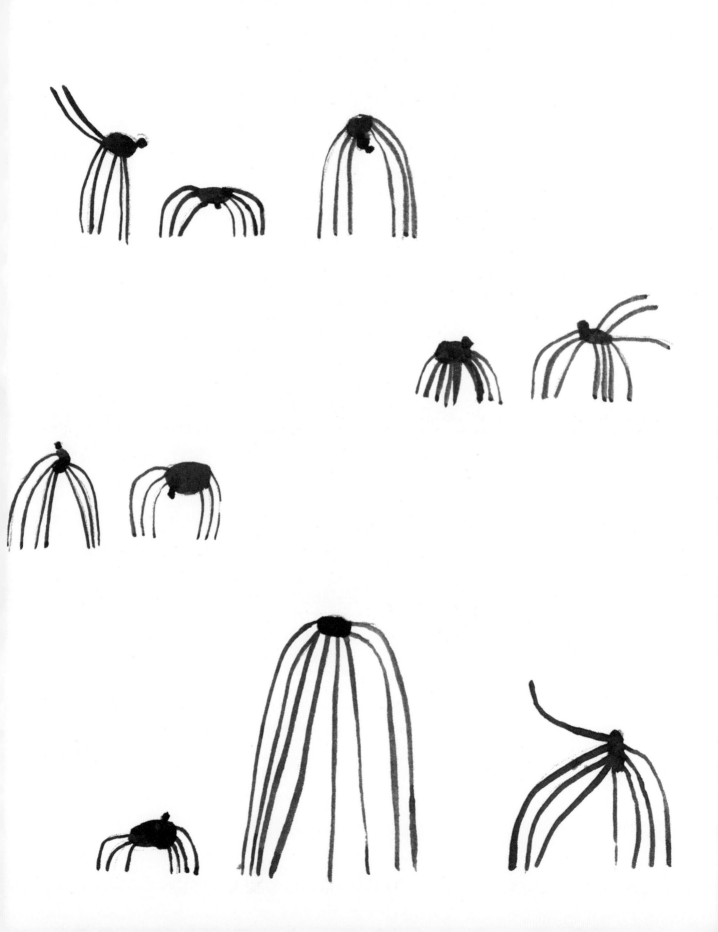

I will have a long dinner table with 19 chairs.

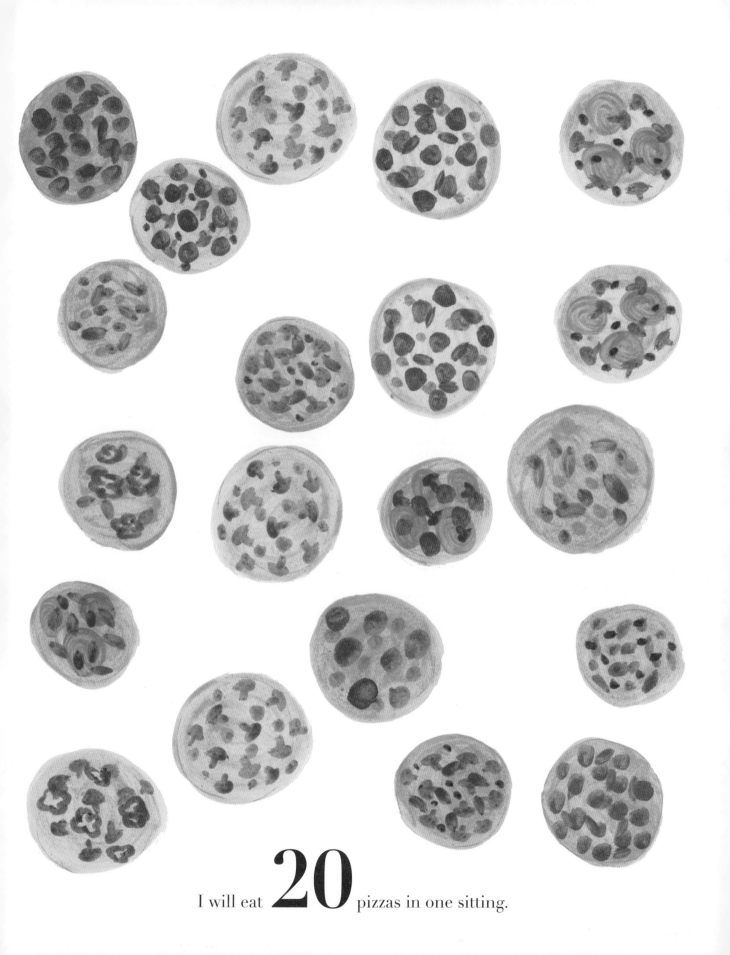

I will eat **20** pizzas in one sitting.

I will feed crumbs to my **21** bird friends. And we will sing together.

I will have a colorful collection of **22** feathers.

I will play hide-and-seek between the **23** houses in my neighborhood.

I will have pillow fights with **24** pillows … every night!

I will go to bed at **25** o'clock.

And in the morning, I will wake up even bigger than the day before!